Timmy's On Time

Anna Maria Prezio, Ph.D.

Copyright © 2024 by Anna Maria Prezio Ph.D.

All rights reserved.

ISBN paperback 978-1-960995-74-2

ISBN hardback 978-1-960995-75-9

ISBN eBook 978-1-960995-76-6

No portion of this book may be reproduced in any form without written permission from the publisher or author, except as permitted by U.S. copyright law.

Dedication

This book is dedicated to my son, Anthony, and my granddaughter, Izabella, to whom I told this story when they were children.

Once upon a time in a cozy little row house on Chestnut Street, there lived an 8-year-old boy named Timmy. He was popular among his friends at school and in the neighborhood.

His bright blue eyes sparkled with curiosity, and he loved playing baseball with his buddies right on their street.

Timmy's parents were wonderful people. His mother, Jane, was a schoolteacher, and his father, Bill, worked as an accountant. They were proud of their son and always encouraged his adventures.

When Timmy got home from school that day, he asked his mother if he could go to Norman's house. As he was getting ready to leave, his mom reminded him, "Don't forget to be back home at 8:00 o'clock." With permission to ride his bike down the street to Norman's house, Timmy promised his mother he would be back by 8:00 PM.

Timmy enjoyed a delicious dinner with his friend Norman and his family.

The boys finished dinner, asked to be excused and went into Norman's room to study their math assignment.

Timmy saw it was getting late and headed for home with time to spare. He was very proud of his promptness. When he arrived home, he saw his parents' friends were there, so he went upstairs to his room without saying anything.

Meanwhile, back at Timmy's house, his mom decided to invite a few friends for dessert and coffee.

Soon, the cozy row house filled with laughter as guests chatted and caught up. Time passed and Timmy's absence went unnoticed as more friends joined the noisy gathering.

Soon, Timmy's mother realized it was after 8 o'clock and became concerned that Timmy had not returned on time. They learned from Norman that Timmy had left earlier than expected. It only took five minutes to ride to Norman's, which worried them even more, so they decided to take action.

More and more people were coming into Timmy's house to see if they could help. There were neighbors, friends, police, and even Norman's mom stopped by to see if she could help.

As you can imagine, the noise level was extremely high. Even someone from the fire department stopped by to see if there is anything they could do to help.

They called the police and soon after, a police officer knocked on their door and told Bill and Jane that they needed to wait twenty-four hours before the police could begin a search. This delay only increased their worries.

Suddenly, a boy's voice shouted, "Hey, what's going on?" It was Timmy's voice. The loud noise woke him from a sound sleep. You see, he had come home on time, but no one noticed. Rather than interrupt the party, he quietly went to his room and fell asleep. No one had checked his room to see that Timmy was home.

The room then erupted into a cheer. Everyone hugged him. He said, "I didn't want to stop your party. You were having such a fun time, and I was so tired, I went upstairs and fell asleep."

His parents hugged Timmy tightly, relieved beyond words. They said, "We're so happy that you are home safe and sound." Timmy smiled and went back to bed.

And so, the row house on Chestnut Street settled down. The noise was replaced by sighs of relief. Timmy drifted back to sleep, knowing that sometimes even a little adventurer needs rest.

The End.

About the Author

Anna Maria Prezio, Ph.D. is a Board-Certified Holistic Psychologist, and Bestselling author. She received her BA in communications from Villanova University, a Business Graduate degree, and a Ph.D. in psychology and holistic wellness. Her expertise is in the communication arts, visual arts, and entrepreneurship.

Printed in the USA
CPSIA information can be obtained
at www.ICGtesting.com
LVHW051044240824
789170LV00004B/75